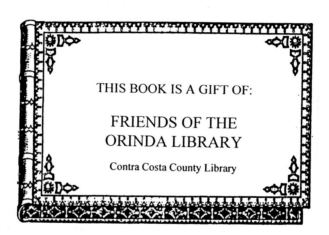

CREATIVE LIVES

FRANK LLOYD WRIGHT

HAYDN MIDDLETON

Heinemann Library
Chicago, Illinois

Customer Service 888-454-2279
Visit our website at www.heinemannlibrary.com

Designed by Tinstar Design
Originated by Ambassador Litho.
Printed and bound in Hong Kong/China

06 05 04 03 02
10 9 8 7 6 5 4 3 2

Library of Congress Cataloging-in-Publication Data
Middleton, Haydn.
  Frank Lloyd Wright / Haydn Middleton.
     p. cm. -- (Creative lives)
Includes bibliographical references and index.
  ISBN 1-58810-203-3
  1. Wright, Frank Lloyd, 1867-1959--Juvenile literature. 2.
Architects--United States--Biography--Juvenile literature. [1. Wright,
Frank Lloyd, 1867-1959. 2. Architects.] I. Title. II. Series.
  NA737.W7 M535 2001
  720'.92--dc21

                              2001000531

Acknowledgments
The author and publishers are grateful to the following for permission to reproduce
copyright material: Frank Lloyd Wright Preservation Trust, pp. 4, 10, 13, 14, 21, 27, 38; Paul
Rocheleau, pp. 5, 19, 20, 23, 41, 47; State Historical Society of Wisconsin, pp. 6, 8, 24, 26, 28,
34, 44, 52; Nancy Stone/Chicago Tribune: p. 9; Alan Weintraub/Arcaid, pp. 15, 16, 54; Natalie
Tepper, pp. 19, 31; Gurdjieff Institute, p. 23; Art Institute of Chicago, p. 29; Lewis
Gasson/Arcaid, p. 33; Frank Lloyd Wright Archives: Associated Press, p. 37; Avery
Architectural and Fine Arts Library, Columbia University, p. 42; Michael Freeman, p. 43;
Kobal, p. 46; John Donat Photography, p. 48; Richard Bryant/Arcaid, p. 50; Chicago
Historical Society, p. 51; John Edward Linden/Arcaid, p. 54.

Lyrics on page 51 copyright (c) 1969 Paul Simon. Used by permission of the Publisher: Paul
Simon Music

Cover photograph reproduced with permission of Corbis.

Special thanks to Frank Lipo for his comments in the preparation of this book.

Every effort has been made to contact copyright holders of any material reproduced in this
book. Any omissions will be rectified in subsequent printings if notice is given to the
publisher.

Some words are shown in bold, **like this.** You can find out what they mean by looking
in the glossary.

CONTENTS

An American Architect ——————————— 4

Childhood ——————————————— 8

First Steps toward Fame —————————— 12

Eye Music ———————————————— 18

Family Ferment ————————————— 24

New Horizons —————————————— 28

Wright against the World ———————— 32

The Great Turnaround ——————————— 40

A National Living Treasure ————————— 44

So Long, Frank Lloyd Wright ——————— 48

Frank Lloyd Wright: The Man and His Work —— 52

Frank Lloyd Wright's Influence ——————— 54

Timeline ———————————————— 56

Glossary ———————————————— 60

Places to Visit —————————————— 62

More Books to Read ——————————— 63

Index —————————————————— 64

AN AMERICAN ARCHITECT

Frank Lloyd Wright will always be remembered as a fine and revolutionary architect. The American Institute of Architects has called him "the greatest American architect of all time." He changed the American house to reflect the new American way of life. Some of his architectural innovations, such as the living room, are standard in houses today.

Frank Lloyd Wright always acted and dressed dramatically. He wanted people to know he was an artist, even if they had not seen his buildings.

Wright was a passionate, patriotic, and hard-working man. He saw himself as a kind of missionary for his own **radical** ideas and principles. Not everyone approved of him or his work, but few doubted that his buildings had a powerful impact on American life. His constant dream was to create a new architecture; one that did not look back to old European models, but instead reflected and celebrated the way that modern American people lived. "Whether people are fully conscious of this or not," he once said, "they actually derive **countenance** and **sustenance** from the atmosphere of the things they live in or with. They are rooted in them just as a plant is in the soil in which it is planted."

"The artist himself, of course, is of his time or he is not an artist. He is the prophet of his time and of his day; he is the seeing-eye of his people. He can see a little further and more clearly than his people see. That's why he's an artist. If he doesn't do that, he is no artist. If he doesn't bring beauty into being they cannot see it by themselves; and that's why he is greater than the conqueror; he is in at the birth of the beautiful, and the conqueror is only the death of the enemy."

Late in his career, Frank Lloyd Wright said this in a speech about what it means to be an artist.

Wright was the architect of this house, Fallingwater, built in Pennsylvania in 1936. It has been called the most famous house ever designed for non-royalty.

A restless genius

Wright lived for almost a hundred years, and he seldom wasted any of his time. He was born just two years after the end of the American Civil War; he died two years after the launching of the first Sputnik satellite into space. In between, he designed 1,141 works. These

Wright's apprentices and admirers understood that he was a great architect. "One felt in the presence of a great man," said Herbert Fritz, a **draftsman.** "He'd either shock you or amuse you. He was 200 percent alive."

"[His neighbors] thought him an **eccentric** visionary because his ideals, and even the house that was our home, were different from theirs. His clients were subjected to ridicule—a 'crazy architect' built 'freak houses' for them."

John Lloyd Wright wrote a book about his father in 1946. It talks about how shocking Wright's houses were at first.

included many houses, hotels, offices, churches, bridges, museums, synagogues, and schools. Though he designed over 1,000 buildings, he only built 532 of them. This is because some people decided they did not like his designs, and chose other, more traditional, architects to build them a house. Of the 532 buildings that Wright built, 409 still stand. One of his lasting achievements was to free Americans from the **Victorian** boxes that were popular in the nineteenth century. He did this by designing **open-plan** houses, with rooms that flowed together and opened into one another.

Wright was obsessed with the idea that buildings should grow naturally from their surroundings. This idea was important to him because he had always been able to see patterns and rhythms in the natural world around him. As a boy, he taught himself to see the branches of trees as natural **cantilevers.** Many years later, he must have had them in mind when he designed the cantilevers for Fallingwater.

Throughout his life, Wright praised the beauty of local, American materials, and worked to create an **organic** kind of architecture, in which the man-made would harmonize with the environment. He urged his apprentices to "study nature, love nature, stay close to nature. It will never fail you." There was no possibility that anything Wright designed would be merely functional. "A building is not just a place to be," he said. "It is a way to be."

But a man with such strong views was bound to upset some people. Wright knew how provocative and aggressive he could be. "I've always wanted to take the dust off people," he once laughed. Even when most people did not agree with him, Wright was confident that he was right, and that they would realize that he was right later. As his son, John, wrote in a biography of his father, called *My Father Who Is on Earth,* "As a young man he had the indispensible quality of confidence in himself. He was ambitious, but his idea of the way to rise was to improve himself." Wright believed that he was right about architecture, but he also knew his architecture would have to be perfect for the rest of the world to understand that he was right.

CHILDHOOD

Frank Lincoln Wright was born in Richland Center, Wisconsin, on June 8, 1867. His father, William Cary Wright, was a musician and a minister in the Unitarian church. He was fourteen years older than his wife, Anna Lloyd-Jones Wright, who was a schoolteacher.

William and Anna were married in either 1865 or 1866. William had been married before he met Anna, but his wife had died. He had three children from his first marriage. Frank was Anna's first child. At the time Frank was born, Anna and William were living in Richland Center, a small town near Spring Green, Wisconsin. Anna's family, the Lloyd-Jones family, lived nearby. The Lloyd-Jones family had moved to Spring Green from Wales in 1844. Wales is one of the nations that makes up Great Britain. Although it has been part of Great Britain for hundreds of years, Wales has a different language, called Welsh, and

The Lloyd-Jones family lived in a Wisconsin farmhouse like this. Wright remembered spending summers on the family's farm.

No one knows exactly where Frank Lloyd Wright was born. We know that the house was in or around Richland Center, Wisconsin. Some experts believe that this house is the house where Wright was born.

different traditions. The Lloyd-Jones family kept their Welsh traditions when they moved to Wisconsin. Frank's grandmother kept the Welsh language, too. She never learned to speak English. The Lloyd-Jones family had a farm in Wales, and they moved to Spring Green because of the good farmland there.

Anna was a young girl when the Lloyd-Jones family moved away from Wales. She made sure her own children knew all the myths and legends from her old country. Wright took his **Celtic** ancestry seriously. He later changed his middle name, Lincoln, to Lloyd, after his mother's family. Wright also named his home Taliesin after a character from an old Welsh myth.

Moving around

Wright's parents had two more children. Jane was born in 1869, and Maginel was born in 1877. Their father moved the family around a lot in his search for work as a musician and preacher. The young Wright spent parts of his boyhood in Rhode Island, Iowa, and Massachusetts. This was not good for his education, and there is no proof that he ever graduated from high school. No matter where the family went, they were usually short of money, and this put a great strain on the relationship between Wright's parents.

When Wright was eleven, the family moved to Madison, Wisconsin. Here they were close to the Lloyd-Joneses. Wright spent each summer on the farm of his uncle, James Lloyd-Jones. "As a boy," he later wrote, "I learned to know the ground plan of the region in every line and feature … I still feel myself as much a part of it as the trees and birds and bees are, and the red barns."

He would never lose his love for this part of the world. But his relatives made him work long hours on the farm. When Wright complained they told him to "add tired to tired." Wright never forgot this saying.

This photo was taken when Wright was ten, just before his family moved to Madison, Wisconsin.

Becoming the head of the household

Wright did not learn much in school, but his mother made sure he made up for it at home. It never crossed her mind that her shy child might not be a genius. She agreed with the educational theories of Friedrich Froebel, who believed that all children were capable of being creative and productive if they were encouraged in the right ways. She bought Wright some "Froebel blocks," cubes, spheres, and cylinders made of wood, which could be fitted together to construct model buildings. With these blocks, which were intended to make children aware of color and shape, Wright made his very first designs. "Those blocks stayed in my fingers all my life," he later said.

His mother also encouraged Wright to learn about the natural world. He had a quiet place in the house to draw, read, and keep the rocks he collected. Wright read a lot, and he was soon reading books like Victor Hugo's *Hunchback of Notre Dame*, which had a chapter on architecture that he especially enjoyed. This pleased his mother because, according to Wright's *Autobiography*, before he was born she had decided how he would show his brilliance: "The boy, she said, was to build beautiful buildings ... she intended him to be an architect."

There is no record of what Wright's father had in mind for him. In 1884, William and Anna's marriage finally fell apart. William moved out and asked for a divorce, which he got in 1885. Wright's son, John, remembered his grandmother telling him about the day his grandfather left. "'You can take your hat and go,' she said to him. 'And do you know what he did?' she asked, tapping me sharply on the knee with her walking stick. 'He walked right over to the hat rack, took his hat, walked politely out the door, and that was the last I ever saw or heard of him.'" Wright never saw his father again. He did not even attend his father's funeral in 1904. From 1884 on, his only family was his mother, his sisters, and the Lloyd-Jones relatives. According to Wright's mother, his father had left her with just one 50-cent piece. Now Wright, at the age of 17, was the head of the household. He had to work to make sure that the family did not sink into poverty.

FIRST STEPS TOWARD FAME

Wright had his mother to thank for his first paid work. She pulled some strings to get him a part-time job as a **draftsman** with Allan D. Conover, a **civil engineer** at the University of Wisconsin. In the mornings he also studied civil engineering at the university. He enjoyed this grounding in both the principles and practice of construction work, and read about art and architecture in his spare time. In 1886, he assisted the architect Joseph Lyman Silsbee with the drafting and building of Unity Chapel. Unity Chapel was the Lloyd-Jones family chapel near Spring Green. But even at this early stage, Wright had itchy feet. In 1887, at the age of 20, he decided to leave small-town America behind and move to a big city: Chicago.

Wright in the Windy City

Wright arrived in the city of Chicago, Illinois, on a drizzly night in 1887. He worked for a year as a draftsman for J.L. Silsbee. This gave him a detailed knowledge of how to design houses. Then the architectural company of Adler and Sullivan gave him a job.

Louis Sullivan, one of the most famous architects of the time, took Wright under his wing. He saw that the younger man was enthusiastic, efficient,

---

Chicago

By the mid– to late nineteenth century, Chicago had become a great city that was home to around a million people. Chicago was located in the middle of America, between the manufacturing East and the farming West. It was connected to the rest of the U.S. by road, rail, river, and lake. Many buildings in the city were made of wood, so when a fire started in October 1871, it spread rapidly, helped by winds blowing from the **prairies**. The Great Fire destroyed the city: 18,000 buildings in an area of 2½ square miles (6.5 square kilometers) burned to the ground. Chicago was quickly rebuilt using brick and stone instead of wood.

---

and already an exceptionally good designer. "He loved to talk to me," Wright later wrote in his *Autobiography*, "and I would often stay listening, after dark, in the offices in the upper stories of the great tower of the Auditorium Building looking out over Lake Michigan, or over the lighted city."

Sullivan had become famous designing new buildings for Chicago after the Great Fire in 1871. He also made his architectural ideas famous by writing about them. He believed that architecture ought to express the spirit of the function of a building. So a waterworks, for example, should not simply function as an efficient pumping machine. Its design should also, somehow, give an impression of flowing water. He coined a famous phrase, **"Form** follows function," which impressed Wright greatly. He also believed strongly that buildings in the U.S. should have a distinctly modern American style, and not an old-fashioned or European appearance.

Wright never forgot how much he learned from Louis Sullivan, shown below, who was his supervisor when he worked for Adler and Sullivan. In 1949, Wright published *Genius and the Mobocracy*, a biography of Sullivan.

Wright worked for Sullivan for six years, steadily increasing his responsibilities. Although his salary also increased, Wright was spending more and more money. He was running up serious debts by playing as hard as he worked. Wright had conquered his youthful shyness, and now he spent a lot of his time and money on parties, going to concerts, and trips to the theater.

13

Catherine L. Wright was a beauty who came very close to Wright's youthful ideal of an "intimate fairy princess" who would inspire him to great deeds and "unquenchable triumphs."

Becoming a family man

Soon after arriving in Chicago, Wright met someone else who would have a profound influence on his life. Catherine Lee Tobin was sixteen when she first met Wright. She married him two years later, on June 1, 1889, when Wright was almost 22. Catherine came from a wealthy Chicago family, had a fine sense of humor, and was devoted to her talented husband. She would often wear clothes that he had designed.

Catherine could be very stubborn. A popular saying in the Tobin family was, "Often in error, but seldom in doubt!" One of Catherine's nieces said of her, "She talked faster than she listened."

"

Wright's son David recalled in later life, "As a family we got along very well, but we were all opinionated and hard on each other. [There were] a lot of criticisms. But we were united against the outside world. Fights? Oh, yes, there were plenty of those. I remember after Dad put us in the dormitory, there was a seven-foot partition dividing the girls' side from the boys', and when our sisters were having slumber parties we would throw a pillow over the partition. It took some skill."

"

Both families disapproved of the marriage. Catherine's family thought she was too young to get married. Anna Wright never found it easy to share her beloved son with another woman. She advised Wright not to marry Catherine, then fainted at the wedding, and went on to make her new daughter-in-law's life difficult in numerous small ways from her home, right next door to the newlyweds' house. Despite their parents' disapproval, Catherine and Frank were happily married, and soon started a family. Their first child was Lloyd, born in 1890; then they had another son, John, born in 1892; followed by Catherine in 1894; David, born in 1895; Frances, born in 1898; and finally Llewellyn, born in 1903.

Oak Park—an early masterpiece

In 1889, with the help of a generous loan from Sullivan, Wright designed a house that was built in Oak Park, a suburb 10 miles (16 kilometers) to the west of Chicago. It still stands today, and is a fine example of

This is the Oak Park home that Wright built for himself in 1889.

Wright's early architectural principles. From the outside it looked quiet and simple, combining dark **shingles** and brick walls with white stone **coping.** The inside was full of oriental rugs, Japanese prints, bowls of flowers, and small sculptures of Wright's favorite composers. Wright left the wood inside unpainted, and did not cover the plaster with wallpaper or paint.

The heart of the house was its fireplace. Families used to spend a lot of time in front of the fireplaces in their homes, and Wright wanted families to have a place to gather in his modern houses, too. From the beginning, fireplaces were an important symbol in the houses he designed. The one at Oak Park was set off from the main room in a small nook, and over the fireplace two inscriptions were carved into a wooden panel. One said: *Truth is Life.* The other said: *Good Friend, Around These Hearth-Stones Speak No Evil Of Any Creature.*

The playroom at Oak Park was added in 1895. Wright designed the large mural over the fireplace based on a tale from *The Arabian Nights*.

"A jolly carnival"

Wright lived in the Oak Park house for 20 years, and he rearranged the house again and again. Ever restless, Wright made changes every six months or so. One major change came in 1898, when he built a studio next door with stained-glass windows that he designed. The studio became his office, and he worked there every day. Although Wright made a lot of changes, he always preserved the house's sense of proportion. He liked to say that he made all his houses to fit a "normal-sized" person. This, naturally, meant a person who was 5 feet 8 inches (174 centimeters) tall—just like himself!

Wright worked extremely hard during his years at Oak Park. He wrote down his ideas very fast, often in finished form. In old age, he would say that he "rolled ideas out of his sleeve" at this point in his life. He liked to draw plans late at night or close to dawn, when the children were asleep. He loved to be in his studio with a blank sheet of paper under a direct white light. There he would set to work with his freshly sharpened colored pencils. When he was working on a design that particularly interested him, Catherine would try to help him work by playing Bach on the piano, or by preparing his favorite meal, baked onions. A servant would keep his fire going in winter, or bring in lemonade during the hot summer months.

Although Wright's children did not see their father often, they remembered the musical evenings he organized for the family. Wright had a talent for cheering up anyone who was unhappy. "Papa would ... laugh them out of it," his son John remembered. "He ... gave our home the feeling of a jolly carnival."

Wright even made intruders feel at home. One night a burglar broke into his Oak Park home. This was not hard to do, since the doors were never locked because Wright did not like to carry keys. Wright heard the burglar, and turned on the lights so that the thief could see what he was stealing. Instead of being angry or afraid, Wright asked the intruder why "so handsome a fellow didn't get out and work in the light where he could be seen and appreciated!"

EYE MUSIC

In 1893, Wright was asked to leave Adler and Sullivan, after Sullivan discovered that Wright had been accepting **commissions** without the company's knowledge. He set up his own architectural **practice** from Oak Park, and worked there until 1909. Wright prepared a full set of **working drawings** every six weeks on average, usually for wealthy professional clients, and many of his designs ended up as actual buildings. Wright had a very exact vision of how the buildings should look; he took control over the details of both the inside and the outside of his buildings. It was obvious right away that Wright was creating a new style. His buildings looked nothing like the buildings around them.

A brand new American style

Wright's first independent commission, when he was 26 years old, was a triumph. William H. Winslow hired Wright to build him a house in River Forest, Illinois. The house is still praised by critics today. Built from simple, natural materials such as Roman brick, cast concrete, and **terra-cotta,** the house was designed in a brand new style that suited the American environment and the modern American way of life. The Winslow house was one of Wright's earliest attempts to create a natural link between a house, the people who lived in it, and the land the house was built on. Later he would refer to this aspect of his work as "**organic** architecture." Wright said that his houses grew naturally out of the needs of the client, the nature of the site, and the kinds of native materials that were available.

Winslow was a wealthy man who was only a little bit older than Wright was when the house was commissioned, and he encouraged Wright to create something modern. From the outside, the house looked very different from the tall, heavily decorated neighboring houses, which were typical of the late **Victorian** period. The sleek, uncluttered interior of Winslow House was also different. Wright wanted the house to create a sense of freedom, rather than follow strict **classical** rules. He referred to this sense of freedom as "continuity in the building itself." He once wrote, "Instead of two things, one thing. Let walls,

Winslow House (top) was built in 1893, in River Forest, Illinois. It looked radically different from the late Victorian houses (bottom) that surrounded it.

ceilings, floors become part of each, growing into one another, getting continuity out of it all or into it all, eliminating any constructed feature."

The prairie house years

For Adler and Sullivan, Wright had specialized in building homes rather than commercial projects, like opera houses or concert halls. In later years, he would win international acclaim for buildings like a great hotel in Tokyo, and a great museum in New York. But at the turn of the century, he became famous building houses. Some people still believe that Wright's houses from the early 1900s were his most original and important buildings.

More than 20 of these **"prairie** houses," or houses built in the "prairie style," still stand in and around Oak Park. Some other Chicago

19

architects made houses in this style, but Wright was the best-known architect in the prairie style. "I loved the prairie," he wrote. "The trees, flowers, and sky were thrilling by contrast ... a little height on the prairie was enough to look like much more. Notice how every detail as to height becomes intensely significant and how breadths all fall short." To match the prairie environment, he believed that people's houses should have long, low, graceful lines, without attics or basements: "I began to see a building primarily not as a cave, but as broad shelter in the open."

Wright's prairie houses are not identical. He made each building fit the land around it, and fit the client's needs. But in every prairie house, Wright wanted to destroy the idea that the house was a box. He made rooms flow into one another by leaving out unnecessary walls and doors. He also put in a lot of windows to open the house up to the landscape. He rejected the idea of treating windows as individual holes cut into walls. Instead, he grouped them together as long, continuous bands of light.

The Ward W. Willits house was built in 1902, in Highland Park, Illinois. It is typical of Wright's prairie style. Wright described the house's appearance, both inside and outside, as "eye music."

Houses on a human scale

Wright wanted his houses to fit the way people lived in them. He refused to make houses with small, stuffy rooms. The biggest rooms in a prairie house are rooms that people would use, like living rooms, dining rooms, and bedrooms. There were no rooms just for show, but all of the rooms were decorated

This picture of Wright was taken in 1905, at the time that he was building prairie houses. He was also working on Unity Temple, his first commission that was not a house.

beautifully, as you can see in the dining room of the Willits House. Until the turn of the twentieth century, houses had been uncomfortable places that were designed to show off the owner's wealth. At the turn of the century, many wealthy, young people were interested in the family. These people were moving from the cities out into the suburbs, so their families could grow up in a better environment. They wanted the places they lived in to reflect their family life, so architects started to design houses as homes. Wright, like other major architects of the early 1900s, was mainly building homes for these young, wealthy, suburban people.

Wright was famous not just for the beauty and modern look of his houses, but also for the amount of buildings he worked on at this time. The **Taliesin Foundation** has listed more than 150 buildings designed by Wright that were constructed during this busy period of his career.

In 1905, Wright was commissioned to design a Unitarian church in Oak Park. This was his first design for something other than a house. Wright wanted the church to be human sized, and not intimidating to people, as medieval cathedrals were. He also made sure that it faced away from the busy street so that people could hear the sermons. The

Arts and Crafts influences

The Arts and Crafts movement developed in Britain in the 1880s. It was a reaction to the mass production introduced by the **Industrial Revolution.** The Arts and Crafts movement wanted to bring back the tradition of using beautiful and useful handcrafted objects instead of machine-made objects that all looked the same. As a young man, Wright was deeply impressed by this movement. He was also interested in the writing of the art critic John Ruskin, who first coined the phrase "**organic** architecture." According to Ruskin, architecture was supposed to improve society, and beauty existed in order "to convey the absolute values upon which a sound society must rest." The architects of the Arts and Crafts movement believed that architecture could improve society. They thought that if architecture and interior design used more handmade objects, factory workers would be more successful, since they would move from the factory to become tradesmen. This would make the world more beautiful and make the workers' lives better. The architects designed houses that were decorated with handmade objects. Wright adopted the Arts and Crafts concept that a building should not contain mass-produced objects. He also used the Arts and Crafts idea that the objects in a house should reflect the house's design.

church was small, but it was beautiful, and it was praised by critics. As his fame grew in the early 1900s, so did Wright's appreciation of his own talents. He started to dress the way he thought a great artist should dress, with a flaring cape and a cane.

In Unity Temple, built in 1905, Wright considered the convenience of the worshippers. He made sure that you could see and hear the minister from every seat in the church.

FAMILY FERMENT

> "*Frank Lloyd Wright placed great faith in the family unit as the essential core of a free* **democracy.** *His mission was to create an architectural environment that would address the individual and the family unit first of all, and then society as a whole.*"
> From *Frank Lloyd Wright: Master Builder* by B.B. Pfeiffer (1997)

Wright had come to fame as a family man. He came from a large, close-knit family himself, and he and Catherine had six children. But by 1909, something was going wrong in Wright's marriage, just as something had gone wrong in his parents' marriage.

"The absorbing, consuming phase of my experience as an architect ended about 1909," he later wrote. "I had almost reached my fortieth year: weary, I was losing grip on my work and even interest in it … I could see no way out. Because I did not know what I wanted, I wanted to go away … Everything, personal or otherwise, bore down heavily on me. Domesticity most of all. What I wanted I did not know. I loved my children. I loved my home. A true home is the finest ideal of man …" But by the time he turned 40, Wright's own true home was no longer Oak Park. In 1909 he left both his family and his architectural **practice** to travel to Europe with another woman.

This is the only known photo of Mamah Borthwick Cheney, the married woman Wright turned to between 1909 and 1914, when he was unhappy in his own marriage.

"A house divided"

The woman was Mamah Borthwick Cheney, the pretty and intelligent wife of a client for whom Wright had built a house in 1904. No one, including Wright himself, could be sure what led him to destroy so much of what he believed in. He claimed that Catherine had become far more interested in the children than in him, and that they had married when they were too young. In a letter to his mother he said that he was "a house divided against itself by circumstances I can not control."

Wright's behavior made the respectable people of Chicago turn against him, and the number of **commissions** he received dropped as a result. But Wright was not the kind of man to admit he had done something wrong. He thought that it was ridiculous for people to stop ordering buildings from him because he had left his wife and children. "It may be that this thing will result in taking my work away from me," he told the *Chicago Tribune* in 1910. "I shall have my buildings to design, of course. But I shall not have as many as I would have if I had been content to live dishonestly ... It will be a misfortune if the world decides not to receive what I have to give."

Catherine was embarrassed and unhappy about Wright's behavior, but she kept hoping that he would come back to live with her and the children in Oak Park after his return from Europe in 1910. When Wright came back to Chicago he decided to stay with Mamah, but Catherine still hoped he would change his mind. In 1912, she confidently predicted to a friend that the affair would be over in two years' time.

Shining brow

Wright enjoyed his trip to Europe, but he also worked hard. While he was there, he worked on a **portfolio** of his work that was published by Ernst Wasmuth in Germany. The "Wasmuth Portfolio" brought him international recognition, and inspired other architects. While Wright and Mamah lived in Fiesole, Italy, he was inspired by seeing the Villa

A house called Taliesin

Taliesin was a hero in old Welsh myths. Taliesin was described as an artist who was able to see past the way things were to see how they would be in the future. In the *Book of Taliesin*, a collection of poems written by the hero, Taliesin says:
"I was a hero in trouble...
I was a leader, with abundance, who saw beyond the present."
Wright thought of himself in the same way.

Medici, a country house that was built on a hillside. Before they even returned to Chicago, Wright was sketching plans for a similar home, studio, and farm to be shared by him and Mamah. About six months after they returned to the U.S., Wright began supervising construction of the house in the valley where he grew up, near Spring Green, Wisconsin. The building was named Taliesin, and in *An Autobiography*, Wright described how the Villa Medici at Fiesole inspired him to build

Wright's house, Taliesin, was named after a Welsh poet who was a hero in the stories Wright's mother told him. The name meant "shining brow."

it: "I saw the hill-crown in back of the house as one mass of apple trees in bloom ... I saw plum trees, fragrant drifts of snow-white in the spring ... I saw the vineyard ... Yes, Taliesin should be a garden and a farm behind a real workshop and a good home."

Taliesin meant "shining brow," and the finished home was wrapped around a hill. It was built from local limestone and cement plaster made with sand from the Wisconsin River. It overlooked water gardens created by damming a nearby stream. The interior had floors paved in limestone, flagstone, or waxed cypress, and the house blended into the landscape. Wright was proud of the way he blended a welcoming home into the land he loved as a boy. He wrote, "Taliesin's order was such that when all was clean and in place its **countenance** beamed, wore a happy smile of well-being and welcome for all. It was intensely human, I believe."

But his home and his happiness would not last very long. On August 15, 1914, Wright was in Chicago, working on another project. On that day, a servant named Julian Carlton set fire to Taliesin's living quarters and killed seven people as they ran to escape the fire. Mamah and her two children were killed in this tragedy.

The symbol Wright designed for his architectural practice was a cross inside a circle inside a square. It was based on old **Celtic** symbols.

NEW HORIZONS

" In his *Autobiographies*, Wright wrote about the effect the Taliesin tragedy had on him: *"The fact remains—until many years after, to turn my thoughts backward to what had transpired in the life we lived together at Taliesin was like trying to see into a dark room in which terror lurked, strange shadows—moved—and I would do well to turn away."* "

After the tragedy, Wright started to rebuild both his life and Taliesin. Although the living quarters had been destroyed, the studio and a small bedroom had survived. From these two rooms, Wright steadily rebuilt his great house on the hill. "Taliesin lived wherever I stood," he once said. But he could not live there again yet, since the memories of his life there with Mamah were too painful. Wright would not be able to live in Taliesin until the late 1920s. He tried to get over his grief by working extremely hard. He rebuilt Taliesin so that it would look similar, but not exactly the same, as the house that had burned down. He also accepted a lot of **commissions** in faraway places. His son, John, had been working as a **draftsman** in California. Wright hired him to come back to Chicago and help him with all of the commissions he was working on.

Wright received many letters of sympathy from complete strangers after the fire. One came from Miriam Noel, a woman two years younger than Wright. She was a

Miriam Noel came into Wright's life in 1914 and finally married him in 1923.

Not everyone liked Wright's Imperial Hotel, in Tokyo: "Fascinating, ingenious and unique are the words that leap to mind … probably equally applicable to a rabbit warren," said one critic.

divorced sculptor who had once lived in Paris. Unlike Wright's other well-wishers, she wrote him a second letter, offering him helpful advice and asking if they could meet. When they met, Wright thought she was beautiful and interesting, and in a short time, Wright and Miriam had started a relationship. But Catherine still hoped that he would return to the family, and she would not allow him to get a divorce.

To Tokyo

From 1916 to 1922, most of Wright's professional energies went into designing the Imperial Hotel in Tokyo. Wright had been fascinated by Japanese art, architecture, and culture since his first visit to Japan in 1905. He had a large collection of Japanese prints. He was honored to receive the commission to design such an important building in the Japanese capital. The completed hotel would, he believed, confirm his stature as an architect of truly global significance.

The construction was not trouble free, however. There was a language barrier between Wright and the Japanese engineers and workmen. And, as with many of Wright's works in progress, costs kept going up.

The owners finally calculated that they had to pay three times the original price that Wright had given them. Wright was worried about the costs going up, and he thought that one way he could control the costs was to hold John's salary. John kept asking for his money, and Wright kept telling him that he would pay him for his work when they returned to Chicago. One day, Wright asked John to go on an errand for him. He wanted John to go and get a check that he was expecting. When John picked up the check for his father, he had it cashed, and he kept the amount of money that his father owed him for his salary, and gave Wright the rest. Wright was furious. He fired John immediately. Wright and his son did not get along for a long time after this. In spite of the money trouble, the first guests were staying in the new lion-colored hotel, made of lava, concrete, and brick, by July 4, 1922.

Wright made the Imperial Hotel look impressive, both inside and outside, but it also had to stand up to Tokyo's frequent earthquakes. In order to make sure the hotel would last, Wright invented a way to absorb shocks by sinking the central supports for the hotel into the earth. He designed the supports to hold up the floor slabs "as a waiter balances a tray on his fingers." It was an unusual method of building a foundation, and even Wright worried about how successfully it would handle actual shocks and earthquakes.

California interlude

While he was working on the Imperial Hotel, Wright and Miriam made several trips back to the U.S. **Commissions** in the Midwest were disappearing, but Wright was becoming popular in California. He thought about setting up a permanent **practice** there, and took on several major assignments. The most important project was a Los Angeles home for Aline Barnsdall. Wright was as creative and detailed as ever. Because the hollyhock was Barnsdall's favorite flower, the house was decorated with **abstractions** of the plant.

When the Tokyo project was finished, Wright and Miriam settled briefly in Los Angeles before returning to Taliesin. In 1922, Catherine finally gave Wright his divorce, and in the following year he married Miriam.

In 1917, Wright designed Hollyhock House for Aline Barnsdall in Los Angeles.

Before their marriage, Wright's mother died and was buried in the cemetery of Unity Chapel in Spring Green. She was proud that her son was an internationally famous architect, just as she had hoped.

On September 1, 1923, the Great Kanto earthquake hit Tokyo, Japan. More than 140,000 people died in the earthquake, and most of Tokyo was destroyed by the earthquake and the fires that it caused. Newspapers printed rumors that the Imperial Hotel was in ruins. "Frank was so wounded [by this news]," Miriam wrote, "I thought he would die that week." A few days after the earthquake, the truth emerged. The hotel was only slightly damaged, and was being used as a home for refugees after the earthquake. Wright's building had survived the most destructive earthquake ever recorded in Japan.

" This telegram brought Wright the news from Tokyo in September 1923: "Hotel stands undamaged as monument of your genius. Hundreds of homeless provided [for] by perfectly maintained service. Congratulations." "

31

WRIGHT AGAINST THE WORLD

Wright and Miriam lived together for barely six months after their marriage. In May 1924, she moved out and left him. Over the next four years they argued bitterly over the divorce **settlement** she was to receive. The media gave a good deal of attention to their disputes. Wright believed Miriam was using various addictive medicines. He was tired of fighting with her, and problems in his professional life were starting to worry him.

A man out of his time?

After his triumphs in Japan and California, Wright came back to Taliesin, and was shocked when he was not immediately overloaded with jobs. He still saw himself as a pioneer for **quintessentially** American architecture. But to many he now seemed old fashioned and uninteresting, and fewer and fewer clients **commissioned** his designs. The worlds of art and architecture had changed greatly in the years since World War I. Wright had once been a revolutionary figure, but now he seemed traditional. Architects like Mies van der Rohe were getting the commissions for university buildings and other public spaces that Wright thought should be his.

A new wave in the arts

In the early twentieth century, the most popular style of architecture was the "International Style." Architects like Le Corbusier, Gropius, and Mies van der Rohe were inspired by the new machine age and mass production. They designed buildings that showed off new technology, such as steel supports that allowed them to make outside walls out of large panes of glass. These architects thought the new materials and the machines that made them were beautiful, and they described the homes they designed as "machines for living."

In his book on Wright's career, *The Architecture of Frank Lloyd Wright,* Neil Levine described Wright's problems this way: "In Europe, his work began to be seen as irrelevant and out of date; and in America, he was now even more of an outsider than before." Wright thought of himself as a modern architect, but he could not bring himself to design buildings in the International Style. Handcrafted objects and buildings designed to match their locations were too important to him. In the mid– to late 1920s, with his insistence on beauty and individuality, he seemed to be an outsider, increasingly out of step with the times.

Wright had grown up with the family motto, "Truth against the World." He was determined to show the world that he was still a great architect, even though his buildings looked very different from the latest style. Wright had always enjoyed challenges, especially when he had a female ally at his side. And, in 1924, he met his most enduring ally of all—Olgivanna Lazovich.

According to the author Daniel Treiber, this remarkable woman had "a personality sufficiently similar to Wright's own to be accepted, but strong enough not to be crushed." Wright came to depend on Olgivanna's support to encourage him as he fought against the International Style, and struggled to continue his work during the difficulties of the **Depression.**

Wright is shown here with Olgivanna Lazovich, his third wife, with whom he had a daughter, Iovanna, in 1925.

The third Mrs. Wright

Wright's relationship with Miriam began with a fire at Taliesin. In a strange coincidence, a second fire destroyed half of the rebuilt Taliesin in 1925, soon after Wright and Miriam's relationship was over. Again, Wright began to rebuild immediately. As he rebuilt Taliesin, he was thinking of the third woman who would share this home.

Wright met Olga Iovanna Lazovich at a ballet performance in Chicago in 1924. She was known as "Olgivanna," a name that came from running her first two names together. Olgivanna was more than 30 years younger than Wright, who was now 57. She came from Montenegro, in the European **Balkans.** With one failed marriage behind her, and a young daughter named Svetlana, she had left her wealthy family to follow Georgei Ivanovich Gurdjieff. Gurdjieff was a teacher who had created a philosophy of spiritual development. His methods ranged from exercise and dance, to **psychological** exercises that were supposed to awaken his followers from "the profound slumber of humankind." Olgivanna believed that Gurdjieff's methods helped her become more aware of the world around her. She wrote a book called *The Struggle Within*, which explained and praised his work. In Wright, she found a man who believed in his ability to change the world as strongly as Gurdjieff did. She married him, and remained his invaluable partner at Taliesin for over 30 years.

Olgivanna (left foreground) with other followers of Gurdjieff. At his command, they all had to stop whatever they were doing, and "wake" from their daily routines.

Frank Lloyd Wrong?

Despite having found true love, the late 1920s were hard times for Wright. The second Taliesin fire cost him $200,000 for repairs. That was a huge sum for a man who was rarely out of debt even when design **commissions** had been flooding in. He also was losing a large amount of money trying to satisfy Miriam in their divorce settlement. When the divorce was finally settled in 1927, Wright was so deeply in debt that a group of his friends had to help him. Although he was depressed about his money problems, on August 25, 1928, Wright married Olgivanna. His new marriage, and the loyalty of his friends, would help him through his problems with money.

Wright's friends would not allow him to go **bankrupt.** They were angry that Wright was known locally as "Frank Lloyd Wrong," because of his family life, and because he was not in high demand as an architect. Wright's friends and clients solved his money problems by incorporating him. This meant that the architect was turned into a **stock company,** and his supporters bought shares in him. The money raised this way was used to pay off his debts, with the understanding that Wright would repay his **investors** out of his future earnings. But as the **Depression** got worse, Wright knew that he could not rely on commissions to make a living.

The new Taliesin community

In August 1932, Wright announced his new way of making a living: the Taliesin Fellowship. He had always had young associates around him in his work, but now Wright began a career as their paid teacher. Trainees would work for him as apprentices in residence, helping to restore the buildings of Taliesin while learning "essential architecture" against a background of "Philosophy, Sculpture, Painting, Music, and the Industrial Crafts." His goal was not only to train good architects, but also to produce responsible, creative, and cultured human beings.

The ambitious program was run as much by Olgivanna as by Wright. To keep it running smoothly, she drew from her experiences as a member of Gurdjieff's community, while Wright tried to create an atmosphere of hard work and admiration of nature that reflected his life as a child.

The Fellowship began on October 1, 1932. All 23 places were filled immediately. Each apprentice had to pay an annual fee of $650, and in the following years students came from all over the globe. Most of them were so thrilled to learn from Mr. Wright that they gladly did the domestic work expected of them at Taliesin. Although Olgivanna once claimed that servants were vulgar, and had no place at Taliesin, some

Princeton principles

In a lecture at Princeton University in the 1930s, Wright listed the rules he used to design buildings. They included:
- reducing the separate rooms to a minimum, and making all of the space inside the building come together;
- associating the building with its location;
- eliminating the idea that rooms and buildings were boxes;
- only using ornament that came from the nature of the building materials or the building's location;
- incorporating the furnishings as "**organic** architecture," so that they reflected the design of the building and had designs that were simple enough that they could be made by machines.

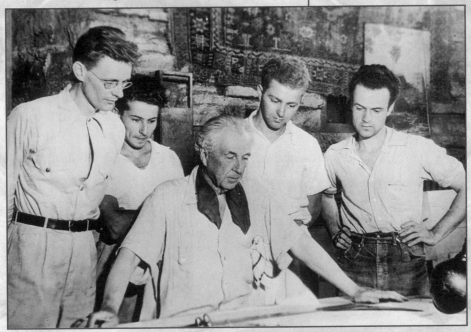

Wright's Fellowship apprentices, at Taliesin in 1938, were "maybe in the kitchen one day, and the next day driving a tractor ... but nearly every day ... in the drawing-office making plans ..."

observers felt that Wright's apprentices were treated as servants, but they had to pay Wright to serve him.

Although he was now over 60 years old, Wright still pushed himself very hard. He had always been out of bed early in the morning, and he often started work hours before breakfast. He claimed that his best ideas came to him out on the farm, in the fields and woods, or beside the stream. "Many times he came to the studio direct from the farm," wrote one of his **draftsmen**, "refreshed and bursting to put new ideas on paper." At other times he came in clutching an envelope, on which he had scribbled down a design that he had come up with in the middle of the night.

He then worked at his drafting board with immense patience and concentration. He went through countless revisions until he felt sure he had captured the "soul" of a projected new building. He could put any personal troubles out of his mind when he worked, and he always entered his studio a happy man. Now and then he would relax by playing Bach or Beethoven on his piano, or lovingly admiring his Japanese prints.

37

But ideas were one thing and clients were another. Some clients could be very demanding, and Wright had to be flexible enough to adapt his designs for them, or politely convince them to change their minds. According to an employee, "He had the highest regard for each of his clients simply because they were his clients; he found virtues in them which were **indiscernible** to others and almost refused to acknowledge their shortcomings." And, as the 1930s wore on, there were more and more clients to deal with. Wright's career was taking off again, even though the **Depression** was at its height.

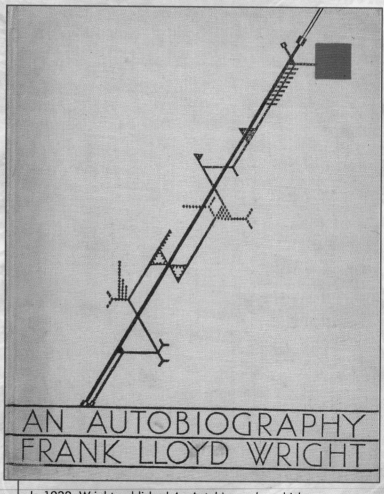

In 1932, Wright published *An Autobiography*, which he dedicated to Olgivanna. He turned increasingly to writing and lecturing in an attempt to make ends meet.

Wright's response to adversity

The Depression had a huge economic impact on all Americans. Wright responded by putting much of his imaginative effort into providing affordable housing for the average American family, and also into **decentralized** planning to relieve crowded cities.

His solutions were the Usonian house and Broadacre City. *Usonian* was a word based on the letters *U* and *S*, which stand for the United States, and it described the kind of architecture that Wright proposed for all over America. His vision included new, cheap methods of house construction, as well as changes in the concept of the residential plan. His main objective was to simplify all aspects of construction, eliminating everything unnecessary—from features to materials.

Wright's 1933 house for Malcolm Willey in Minneapolis put these idealistic principles into practice. And, during the 1930s, Wright's clients did tend to come from less wealthy ranks of society than before. The Broadacre City project was born at Taliesin at a time when hardly any commissions were coming into the office. Wright assigned the apprentices of the Taliesin Fellowship to assist him in designing this idealistic model, which was finally exhibited across the U.S.

Broadacre City

In the words of B.B. Pfeiffer, Broadacre City implemented Wright's ideas about decentralization, "moving the vital components of the overcrowded city into the healthy environment of the country and redesigning the architecture required by such a Usonian community so that the buildings would enhance the life of its citizens and also become integral features of the natural landscape." It got its name from Wright's idea that the city should be spread out, so that each householder could live on an acre of land on which most of the family's food could be grown.

THE GREAT TURNAROUND

"Wright's surge of creativity after two decades of frustration," wrote Robert Twombly in his biography of the architect, "was one of the great **resuscitations** in American art history, made more impressive by the fact that Wright was 70 years old in 1937." Frank Lloyd Wright had not lost his self-confidence. He believed that some of his finest work was still to be done. Everyone who thought he was old fashioned, and that his best work was history, was shocked as he entered one of his most creative periods in his seventies.

From 1932 until Wright's death in 1959, the Fellowship made it possible for Wright to produce a great deal of work. His production team was a group of six permanent Fellowship members. They helped to train new apprentices, to complete studio drafting work, and to represent Wright at various sites around the country. As it happened, there was a sudden increase in **commissions.** This was because Wright's designs were fashionable again, as a result of two buildings that he designed in the mid–1930s.

The house in the waterfall

If a single building restored Wright's reputation, it was the home he designed for Edgar J. Kaufmann in Bear Run, Pennsylvania, between 1934 and 1935. Kaufmann was the wealthy owner of a successful Pennsylvania department store. He had sent his son to be a student at Taliesin Fellowship, so when he wanted an architect to design a vacation house for his family, he asked Frank Lloyd Wright to do the job. Fallingwater, as the Kaufmann house was called, deserved its name. The house sat immediately above a waterfall. Wright wanted the Kaufmanns "not simply to look at the waterfalls, but to live with them." The house he built them represented perhaps his most harmonious match between man and nature.

The house was anchored into the cliff ledges and had three levels, each with its own terrace, with outside stairways leading to more terraces. It was a fantasy of reinforced concrete, local stone, expansive glass windows, and French doors, and the whole concept was

At Fallingwater, wrote Wright, "nature and art were made to complement one another." Even the windows at the far end of the living room were designed to make the scenery outside look like a series of paintings.

suggested by the house's environment. Wright even incorporated into his design a large boulder that the family used to picnic on; it became the hearthstone for the fireplace.

Fallingwater has been called "the most significant residence built in the United States." Soaring in all directions, the house seems to defy gravity. And its **cantilevers,** echoing branches in the surrounding trees, defy modern ideas about safety, too. In 1992, a structural engineer remarked that "there is not a city in the United States, even today, some 57 years later, where one could obtain a building permit to erect Fallingwater." But out in the remote Pennsylvania countryside in the mid–1930s, Wright got away with it. He was justly proud of his achievement, and it may be no accident that his favorite way of signing his own initials, "FLLW," appears in the name of this landmark triumph in his long career: FaLLingWater.

In this photo, Wright and Edgar J. Kaufmann, who commissioned Fallingwater, are shown sitting in Wright's "desert camp," Taliesin West, in Arizona, where he escaped each harsh Wisconsin winter.

The desert camp

Wright's second masterpiece of the 1930s was Taliesin West, built in the western desert of Arizona. Wright had first spent time there in 1927, as a consultant for the Arizona Biltmore Hotel. Then, in 1934–35, he brought part of the Fellowship there to work on his models for Broadacre City. He became so attached to the region that he decided to build a headquarters there for the winter months.

The new home and workshop was camp-like at first and intended only for winter use. But as Wright returned each season with his family and apprentices, he planned for the buildings to become more permanent.

> "I was struck by the beauty of the desert, by the dry, clear sun-drenched air, by the stark geometry of the mountains— the entire region was an inspiration in strong contrast to the lush ... landscape of my native Wisconsin. And out of that experience ... came the design for these buildings. The design sprang out of itself ..."
>
> Wright always said that the landscape in which it was set created the design of Taliesin West.

The building was made of desert stones set into concrete made from local sand. Its walls were set up at odd sloping angles, reflecting the slopes of the nearby mountain ranges. Taliesin West was influenced by the archaeological **excavations** that Wright and some of the apprentices had seen during their 1934–35 trip to Arizona. Wright was fascinated by the Native American architecture that he saw on that trip. The Hohokam and Hopi people had once lived in the area, and Wright named his study in Taliesin West the kiva, after the round rooms the Hopi used for ceremonies.

Like the reconstructed Taliesin in Wisconsin, Taliesin West was built by the Fellowship apprentices. Outside the new building, the desert landscape stayed entirely untouched. As Wright once wrote: "When **organic** architecture is properly carried out no landscape is ever outraged by it, but is always developed by it. The good building makes the landscape more beautiful."

"It is indeed ironic," commented B.B. Pfeiffer, an author who was once an apprentice for Wright, "that America's greatest architect would live in two homes built by young men and women in the act of learning the art of architecture."

The pavilion at Taliesin West was built and maintained by apprentices. For over 20 years it served as Wright's architectural laboratory. It was here that Wright tested design innovations, structural ideas, and building details.

A NATIONAL LIVING TREASURE

When World War II broke out in 1939, Wright was 72 years old. He was in the public eye again; he was featured on the cover of *Time* magazine in 1938, and in the same year a whole issue of *Architectural Forum* was dedicated to his work. Even so, not even Wright could have guessed that he had two more successful decades ahead of him.

Johnson Wax Administration Building

This is the interior of the building that Wright completed in 1939 for S.C. Johnson and Son, a company that made wax products in Racine, Wisconsin. He planned to support the main workroom's skylighted roof with 24-foot concrete columns shaped like lily pads with slender stems. The building license authorities doubted that each column could support its calculated load of 6 tons. Wright decided to do a public test on a sample column. In front of huge crowds, he directed a crane to drop ton after ton of scrap metal onto it. It supported 6 tons, and Wright directed the crane to keep going. The column finally crumpled under a weight of 60 tons. When the building opened, 30,000 people went through it in the first two days.

They admired features like chairs with inwardly leaning backs, that gently urged sitters out of their seats, and a round elevator from which people could see the main floor as they rode up to the next level.

An almost humble hero

Wright was extremely busy in the 1940s. Medals, **honorary doctorates**, titles, and **citations** rained down on him. His private life was no longer of more interest to people than his career. His huge body of work, and his harsh opinions about other architects' work made him the most prominent architect in the U.S., where he was called "a national living treasure." But how did this great change of fortune affect the man himself? Wright said, "somehow I expected each honor would add a certain luster, a certain brightness to the psyche which is mine. On the contrary ... it casts a shadow on my native arrogance, and for a moment I feel coming on that disease which is recommended so highly, of humility."

However, an incident from 1937 shows the great man in his true colors. When greater fortune came his way, Wright built up an impressive collection of cars to use for traveling between the two Taliesins. When the first Lincoln Continental cars came on the market, Wright took his secretary, Gene Masselink, and an assistant to a dealership in Chicago. The assistant later recorded: "Mr. Wright went up to the new Lincoln, tapped the fender with his stick and said, 'I want one of these and one of these. Gene, show him the color we want.' The salesman explained that the color would have to be specially ordered. 'And,' Wright continued, 'I want a convertible top. Take that thing off. I will send you my own design—something like a rolltop desk.' Then he declared, 'and I don't expect to pay for them.' He turned toward the door and added, 'I expect them to be ready in two weeks.'"

Usonian Automatic

Not all architects' designs end up being built. Sometimes the person who is building a home does not care for the architect's design, or the design would cost too much to build. In the mid-twentieth century Wright made many designs, including hospitals, opera houses, and universities, that were never built. As Chicago celebrated a Frank Lloyd Wright Day, there was even a plan for "Mile High Illinois," a sword-like building housing 100,000 people in no fewer than 528 **stories.** This

The *Fountainhead*, a movie directed by King Vidor, starred Gary Cooper as an individualistic and idealistic architect, similar to Wright.

was ironic, since Wright had fiercely attacked the concept of the skyscraper for years.

In 1943, Ayn Rand wrote a best-selling novel, *The Fountainhead*, which soon became a movie starring Gary Cooper. Few missed the similarities between the career of the architect hero and that of Frank Lloyd Wright. Wright himself saw them, commenting that the film was "a grossly abusive caricature of my work." As his fame grew, Wright became even more familiar to Americans on the TV screen. He was a natural in front of the camera.

Wright seemed destined mainly to be a residential architect. Believing that the artist must always serve society, it seemed natural to him to concentrate on society's most essential unit: the home. So he persisted with his dream of providing moderate-cost, single-story Usonian homes for **middle-class** Americans. These had features like heat made by running hot water through pipes in the cement-slab floor, prefabricated walls made of board and cheap tar paper, **open-plan** interiors, and, reflecting a change in American society, garages. In 1954, Wright published a book, *The Natural House*, in which he described a new concept—Usonian Automatic.

This was a do-it-yourself home Wright invented to help people avoid construction costs. In the 1920s, in southern California, Wright had experimented with large concrete blocks that could be used to build a house quickly. Now he produced molds for blocks just one foot by two feet in size: small enough for a single person, ideally the client, to work with. Wright showed how the blocks could be used by designing an elegant home for Gerald B. Tonkens in Amberly Village, Ohio. The Tonkens home is still standing today. Its construction was supervised by Wright's apprentice and grandson, Eric Lloyd Wright.

The Tonkens family was happy with their home but around 1950, the U.S., or at least its building industry, was not ready for Usonian Automatic. People were intimidated by the thought of building a house using the blocks, and Wright had to accept relative failure in this project. Harder by far to bear was a family tragedy which struck in 1946. On the road to Spring Green from Taliesin, Wright's stepdaughter Svetlana and her son were killed in a car accident that seemed to involve no other vehicle.

In 1946, Wright was **commissioned** to design a Unitarian Meeting House in Shorewood Hills, Wisconsin. At Olgivanna's suggestion he designed the roof to represent hands held together in prayer.

47

SO LONG, FRANK LLOYD WRIGHT

Wright was a practicing architect for 72 years. During his last sixteen years, he designed nearly 500 projects, almost half his lifetime output. These are amazing statistics, and proof of his creative energy. Several international exhibitions celebrated his achievement. The most important of these exhibitions was "Sixty Years of Living Architecture," which opened in Florence, Italy, in 1951, and concluded its run at Wright's Hollyhock House in Los Angeles, California, in 1954.

He continued to write, publish, give speeches, and dream. In 1957, his ninetieth year, when 59 new projects came into his studio, he traveled to Baghdad, Iraq, to discuss plans for an opera house and other buildings with the ruling Shah. The talks came to nothing, because the country was turned upside down by a revolution in 1958. In that year, 31 more **commissions** came in, raising the number of ongoing projects in the studio to a breathtaking 166.

When people asked him, "What is your greatest work?" he had always replied "The next one." But to many, his greatest work of all was his last building. This was the museum he designed in New York City for Solomon R. Guggenheim. The museum was under construction from 1943 until six months after Wright's death.

By 1956, Frank Lloyd Wright was famous as an architect and as a critic of other people's architecture. He tried to avoid photographers in later life because "they all make me look like an old woman."

In his book about the Guggenheim Museum, Wright claimed that the strange shape of the building was inspired by the wishes of his client: *"Mr. Guggenheim wanted his people to see a picture much as the artist himself saw it in changing light, and as whoever owned it might see it. He wanted a home for these paintings ... not only to be seen but enjoyed."*

"A beautiful, uninterrupted symphony"

Wright's later masterpieces such as Fallingwater and the Marin County Civic Center proved that he was an ingenious engineer as well as a great designer. He had completely replaced the old box concept of **post-and-beam** construction with a strong sense of the **"plastic."** In a book about the Guggenheim Museum, published in 1960, Wright wrote: "Here for the first time architecture appears plastic, one floor flowing into another (more like sculpture) ... The whole building, cast in concrete, is more like an eggshell—in form a great simplicity— rather than like a crisscross structure. The net result of such construction is a greater **repose,** the atmosphere of the quiet unbroken wave: no meeting of the eye with abrupt changes of form. All is as one."

The Guggenheim Museum's structure, molded into **curvilinear** form, was cast in concrete reinforced with **filaments** of steel. As ever, the building's form was dictated by its function: to present Guggenheim's collection of paintings by modern artists such as Kandinsky, Mondrian, and Leger to the public. Wright's goal was to make a single "beautiful, uninterrupted symphony" out of the building and the paintings on show inside it. But his design was so **radical** that he had to fight with the museum and city authorities for thirteen years before they accepted it.

Does the Guggenheim do its job?

Wright intended the visitor to take an elevator to the top of the single, spiralling ramp and begin a slow descent, admiring the paintings on the inner walls. These walls slope gently back, so the viewer sees the paintings as they would appear if they were still mounted on easels.

A continuous band of skylights and artificial light sources illuminate the art. To supervise the construction of the museum, Wright moved into an apartment at the New York Plaza Hotel, redecorated it entirely, and called it "Taliesin the Third." Before, during, and after construction, a debate raged about whether or not the building was suitable for housing paintings. Some critics were impressed by the attention Wright paid to the way paintings would appear in the Guggenheim, while others believed Wright's design would always detract attention from the paintings themselves. This debate has never stopped.

Two final resting places

After he finished the Guggenheim Museum plans, Wright was in great demand as an architect. He was working on a design for a new state capitol for Arizona, an auditorium building for Arizona State University, and an auditorium building for Madison, Wisconsin. He also was designing a new chapel for the Wisconsin Taliesin that would replace the old Lloyd-Jones chapel. He was planning for this new chapel to have a place where he and Olgivanna would be buried. Frank Lloyd

Wright is shown here at a musical evening at home. Ten years after his death, Wright inspired songwriter Paul Simon to write, "So Long, Frank Lloyd Wright":
Architects may come and
Architects may go and
Never change your point of view.
When I run dry
I stop awhile and think of you.

Wright died peacefully on April 9, 1959, after an operation on his intestines. He was buried at Taliesin, but 26 years later, after the death of Olgivanna, his remains were **exhumed,** cremated, and then sent west to Arizona to be with those of his third wife. "Daddy gets cold up there in Wisconsin," his daughter Iovanna remarked. Some members of his Wisconsin family were not so sure, and strongly disapproved of disturbing him. The newspapers picked up this story and revealed it to the public. Even in death, Frank Lloyd Wright was able to cause a controversy.

FRANK LLOYD WRIGHT: THE MAN AND HIS WORK

In the late 1920s, Isabelle Doyle worked at the State Bank of Spring Green. She also worked as a secretary at Taliesin in the evenings. One day, Frank Lloyd Wright swept into the bank in his artist outfit, wearing a Stetson hat and swinging a cane. Ms. Doyle remembered the bank manager looking Wright up and down and saying, "You certainly look comfortable." Wright replied, "You could do this if you weren't so strait-laced." Only then did she look down and realize that Wright was not wearing any shoes. That was Wright at his most typical: a self-confident artist.

An ultimate nonconformist

"Whoso would be a man," wrote the author Ralph Waldo Emerson, "must be a **nonconformist.**" Wright lived this idea to the fullest. Born into a family of religious nonconformists, he seldom agreed with the majority view in any other area of life. He had his own vision of how life should be lived, and of how buildings should be designed and built. It was not always a vision that other people shared, or that he cared to explain. In her 1992 biography of Wright, Meryle Secrest wrote of his work: "Nothing about Wright's buildings is conceivable at first glance, as if he felt that the hidden treasure at their core was a prize that must be won."

Wright is shown here seated in his study at Taliesin, where he designed many of his masterpieces.

> " *"A great architect is not made by way of a brain nearly so much as he is made by way of a cultivated, enriched heart. It is the love of the thing he does that really qualifies him in the end. And I believe the quality of love is the quality of great intelligence, great perception, deep feeling."* "
>
> Wright said this to the Fellows at Taliesin toward the end of his life.

Wright's vision required a huge amount of self-confidence, especially when he was not understood. In fact, the harder the challenge, the more inspired Wright became to succeed. Then he could draw not only on his great talent, but also on his great energy—his love for what he called "the old gospel of hard work: adding tired to tired." As he grew older, none of this changed. "A creative life is a young one," he said on his 80th birthday, adding, with his usual sense of mischief: "What makes you think that 80 is old?"

Ignoring the next thing

The philosopher Bertrand Russell once wrote, "As men grow more industrialized and regimented, the kind of delight that is common in children becomes impossible to adults, because they are always thinking of the next thing, and cannot let themselves be absorbed in the moment. This habit of thinking of the 'next thing' is more fatal to any kind of **aesthetic** excellence than any other habit of mind."

Wright agreed with Russell, and refused to look too far ahead. This got him into some financial and personal troubles. But he never lost his capacity to be "absorbed in the moment," or express himself joyfully through his creativity. "The purpose of the universe is to play," he said. "The artists know that, and they know that play and art creation are different names for the same thing."

FRANK LLOYD WRIGHT'S INFLUENCE

Frank Lloyd Wright worked to create an architecture that was truly American, and reflected the culture and the landscape of the country. He helped to give other architects the confidence to design in an **indigenous** American style. But through his designs, his writings, his talks, and the hundreds of apprentices who passed through the Fellowship, his ideas became influential all over the world. Throughout his career he had critics as well as fans. Some believed that after World War I his **"organic"** concepts no longer had place in modern architecture. Other critics felt Wright's work was too "personal." Some thought Wright's passion for unity could be overwhelming; and when Wright took a **motif** like a triangle and applied it to every aspect of his design, one critic said, "One's eye vainly seeks relief from this almost obsessive repetition."

Many people ridiculed Wright's apprenticeship system at Taliesin: "Never," went a joke, "have so many people spent so much time

Wright's Marin County Civic Center of 1957 (right) was an attempt to blend government buildings with California hills, making full use of new technology and materials. To him, **classic** structures like the Lincoln Memorial (left) had no place in the U.S. because classic architecture "is related to the toga and the civilization that wore it."

Wright's influence on the Europeans

Wright was not ignored by European architects of the International Style, even though their ideas could seem very different from his. The Swiss architect Le Corbusier wrote in 1925: "the sight of several [of his] houses in 1914 strongly impressed me. I was totally unaware that there could be in America an [architecture] ... so purified and so innovative ... Wright introduced order, and he imposed himself as an architect." In Vienna, Richard Neutra claimed that, "Whoever he was, Frank Lloyd Wright, the man far away, had done something momentous and rich in meaning." Some critics also believed Wright's work helped pave the way for the Art Deco style introduced in Paris in 1925, which featured geometrical and angular designs and decorative motifs.

making a very few people comfortable." But despite his unconventional methods, Wright took his teaching seriously. Olgivanna, with an eye to the future, made sure of that. "It is not enough to build monuments, Frank," she once told him, "now you must build the builders of monuments."

Passing on the principles

Wright's theories had a major effect on modern architecture and the way it is seen. His principles, rather than any particular style, have had the biggest impact. In 1940, the *New York Times* remarked that his main ideas, first expressed in the late 1800s, were both ahead of their time and timeless: "Simplicity, **repose,** individuality; adaptation of the building to its owner, its purposes and its environment; bringing out 'the nature of the materials'; use of the machine to do the work it can do well; sincerity, integrity—these are virtues of architecture now as they were, or should have been, then."

As for Wright himself, he rarely doubted his own significance. Once, asked a question in court, he referred to himself as the world's greatest architect. When someone pointed out that this was not very modest, he replied, "Well, I was under oath, wasn't I?"

TIMELINE

1867	Frank Lloyd Wright is born in Richland Center, Wisconsin, on June 8.
1869–77	Wright's family moves from town to town as his father seeks work.
1878	The Wright family moves to Madison, Wisconsin. Wright starts to spend summers at James Lloyd-Jones' farm.
1885	Wright's parents divorce, and his father leaves Madison. Wright takes a part-time job as a **draftsman** for engineer Allan D. Conover.
1886	Wright attends the University of Wisconsin.
1887–89	Wright leaves Madison for Chicago, becoming a designer for J.L. Silsbee, then goes to work for Adler and Sullivan.
1889	Wright marries Catherine Lee Tobin, and designs a home for them to share in Oak Park, Illinois.
1890	Wright's son Lloyd is born.
1892	Wright's son John is born.
1893	Wright leaves Adler and Sullivan to open his own **practice.** He designs a house and stables for William H. Winslow, in River Forest, Illinois.
1894	The first exhibition of Wright's work is held at the Chicago Architectural Club. Wright's daughter Catherine is born.
1895	Wright's son David is born.
1896	Wright writes the lecture "Architecture, Architect, and Client." The "Romeo and Juliet'" Windmill Tower is designed for Spring Green, Wisconsin.
1897	Wright moves his office to Steinway Hall, Chicago.
1898	Wright's daughter Frances is born.
1901	Wright delivers his lecture "The Art and Craft of the Machine" in Chicago, and designs a house for Ward W. Willits in Highland Park, Illinois.
1902	Wright designs a house for Susan Lawrence Dana in Springfield, Illinois.
1903	Wright's son Llewellyn is born.
1904	Wright's father dies. Wright does not attend the funeral. Wright designs Unity Temple in Oak Park, Illinois, and the Larkin Building in Buffalo, New York, considered by many to be the first modern office building in the U.S.

1905	Wright and Catherine travel to Japan, and Wright becomes an expert in collecting Japanese prints.
1906	Wright designs a house for Frederick C. Robie in Chicago.
1908	Wright designs a house for Avery Coonley in Riverside, Illinois.
1909	Wright leaves his family to travel in Europe with Mamah Borthwick Cheney and work on the Wasmuth **Portfolio** of his work, published in Berlin.
1911	Wright returns to the U.S. and begins to build Taliesin near Spring Green, Wisconsin.
1912	*The Japanese Print: An Interpretation* is published.
1913	Wright visits Japan to secure a **commission** for the Imperial Hotel, Tokyo. Wright designs Midway Gardens in Chicago.
1914	Mamah Cheney and six others are killed as a servant destroys Taliesin in Wright's absence; rebuilding begins after a month. Wright meets Miriam Noel.
1916	Wright travels to Japan with Miriam and opens an office in Tokyo to supervise the construction of the Imperial Hotel.
1917	Wright designs Hollyhock House for Aline Barnsdall, in Los Angeles, and tries for more commissions in southern California.
1922	Wright returns from Japan and opens a Los Angeles office. Wright and Catherine are divorced.
1923	Wright's mother dies, the Imperial Hotel survives a major Tokyo earthquake, and Wright marries Miriam Noel. Wright designs a house for John Storer in Los Angeles.
1924	Wright and Miriam separate. Wright meets Olgivanna Lazovich.
1925	A second fire occurs at Taliesin, and is followed by rebuilding. Wright and Olgivanna's daughter, Iovanna, is born.
1926	The Bank of Wisconsin takes ownership of Taliesin, to cover Wright's debts. Wright starts work on *An Autobiography*.
1927	Wright and Miriam are divorced, and Wright and Olgivanna spend the winter in Arizona as he works on Arizona Biltmore Hotel.
1928	Wright and Olgivanna are married.

1930 Wright delivers the Kahn lectures at Princeton University, which are published as *Modern Architecture* in 1931.

1931 An exhibition of Wright's life work travels to New York, Amsterdam, Berlin, Frankfurt, Brussels, Milwaukee, and Chicago.

1932 Wright founds the Taliesin Fellowship and begins work on building the Fellowship Complex at Taliesin.
An *Autobiography* and *The Disappearing City* are published.
Wright's work is included in the "International Style Exhibition" at the Museum of Modern Art in New York.

1933 Wright designs a house for Malcolm Willey in Minneapolis, Minnesota.

1934 Wright and apprentices begin the Broadacre City model.
Taliesin magazine and Taliesin Press are founded.

1935 Wright designs Fallingwater house for Edgar J. Kaufmann in Bear Run, Pennsylvania.

1937 Wright begins the design and construction of Taliesin West, near Phoenix, Arizona, and designs Wingspread House for Herbert F. Johnson in Racine, Wisconsin.

1938 Wright produces a plan for Florida Southern College in Lakeland, Florida.

1939 Wright completes the Johnson Wax Administration Building in Racine, Wisconsin.
World War II begins.

1940 "The Work of Frank Lloyd Wright," a major exhibition, is held at the Museum of Modern Art in New York.
Wright founds the Frank Lloyd Wright Foundation.

1941 Wright is made an honorary member of the Royal Institute of British Architects, and receives a Royal Gold Medal for Architecture from King George VI.

1942 Wright is made an honorary member of the National Academy of Architects in Uruguay, and designs the Industrial Arts Building for Florida Southern College in Lakeland, Florida.

1943 Wright proposes a design for the Solomon R. Guggenheim Museum in New York.

1945 Wright designs the Administration Building for Florida Southern College in Lakeland, Florida.

1946 Wright's stepdaughter Svetlana dies in a car accident. Wright designs the Unitarian Meeting House in Shorewood Hills, Wisconsin, and the Johnson Wax Research Tower in Racine, Wisconsin.

1947 Wright receives an **honorary doctorate** of fine arts from Princeton University.

1948 The January issue of *Architectural Forum* is dedicated to Wright's work.

1949 Wright publishes *Genius and the Mobocracy* about Louis Sullivan, and is made an honorary member of the American National Institute of Arts and Letters and awarded the Gold Medal of the American Institute of Architects.

1950 Wright is awarded an honorary doctorate of law by Florida Southern College in Lakeland, Florida.

1951 Wright and his apprentices design and construct an exhibition called "Sixty Years of Living Architecture," which opens in Florence, Italy.

1953 Wright publishes *The Future of Architecture*. Wright is made an honorary member of the National Academy of Finland.

1954 Wright designs Beth Sholom Synagogue in Elkins Park, Pennsylvania. An apartment in the Plaza Hotel in New York is remodeled for Wright to live in.

1955 Wright opens an office and residence in New York City, called Taliesin the Third, and designs the Dallas Theater Center in Texas.

1956 *The Story of the Tower* is published. October 17 is declared Frank Lloyd Wright Day in Chicago, and Wright presents "Mile High Illinois" at the Chicago exhibition. Construction work begins on the Guggenheim Museum.

1957 Wright travels to Baghdad, Iraq to discuss a new project, and designs Marin County Civic Center and Post Office in San Rafael, California.

1959 Wright starts work on a history of architecture for teenagers, called *The Wonderful World of Architecture*. Wright dies on April 9. The Guggenheim Museum opens in October.

GLOSSARY

abstraction artistic representation of a thing that does not try to show it realistically

aesthetic to do with the appreciation of beauty

Balkans southeastern part of Europe including Bosnia, Croatia, Bulgaria, and Albania

bankrupt having no money or anything of value to pay a debt

cantilever long bracket or projecting beam fixed at one end, for example in a wall, to support a structure, such as a balcony

Celtic name for the original people who inhabited Scotland, Ireland, Wales, Cornwall, and Brittany, and their culture

citation official recognition of achievement

civil engineer someone who plans and builds roads, docks, and many other public buildings and structures

classical characteristic of the art of ancient Greece or Rome

commission agreement by a person to pay for a job to be done

coping top row of stone in a wall

countenance to approve something, or an expression of the face

curvilinear consisting of curved lines

decentralized to move things away from the center

democracy/democratic type of society where everyone has a say in the running of the country by electing the government

Depression economic slump that began in 1929, when money dropped in value leading to mass unemployment

draftsman someone who makes drawings or sketches, in this case of buildings

eccentric type of behavior that is not considered normal, or person who demonstrates that unusual behavior

excavation hole that is dug in the ground

exhume to dig up from a place of burial

filament thread, fiber

form shape and structure

honorary degree/doctorate educational qualifications offered out of respect, without the receiver having to go to class or be graded

indigenous belonging to or originally inhabiting a region or locality

indiscernible invisible, impossible to make out

Industrial Revolution name given to the period between about 1750 and 1850 in which machinery came to replace human labor

investor person who spends money on a project hoping it will make them more money

middle class section of society between the working class and the rich

motif repeated theme, subject, or figure

nonconformist not believing or behaving like most others, often in religious matters

open plan building with few inside walls

organic in architecture, a building that fits in naturally with its natural surroundings, yet forms a complete whole within itself

plasticity/plastic fluidity, lack of straight lines and right angles in a building

portfolio published edition of an architect's plans and drawings

post-and-beam traditional, non-plastic, form of building, with vertical walls supporting horizontal parts

practice professional business or company

prairie treeless stretch of grassland

psychological having to do with the mind or beliefs

quintessential purest or most typical form of something

radical extreme, wanting changes from the way things are

repose rest, relaxation

resuscitation revival

settlement in a divorce, an agreed financial arrangement

shingle rectangular piece of wood like a tile, used on roofs and the sides of buildings

stock company business that people are able to buy parts of; they then receive a share of the business profits

story floor or level of a building

sustenance something that makes you strong and healthy

Taliesin Foundation established by Wright in 1940 following the formation of the Taliesin Fellowship in 1932. The Foundation preserves Wright's works and continues to provide opportunities to study organic architecture.

terra-cotta brownish-red fine clay used to make building materials among other things

Victorian term describing the period that covers the reign of Queen Victoria in Britain, which lasted from 1837 until her death in 1901

working drawing detailed drawing that shows builders how they should construct a building

PLACES TO VISIT

Fallingwater
Bear Run, Penn. 15464
Pennsylvania Route 381 between Mill Run and Ohiopyle
724-329-8501

Florida Southern College
Child of the Sun Visitor Center
Lakeland, Fla. 33801
863-680-4110

Frank Lloyd Wright Home and Studio
951 Chicago Ave.
Oak Park, Ill. 60302
708-858-1976

Guggenheim Museum
1071 5th Avenue at 89th Street
New York, N.Y. 10017
212-423-3500

Johnson Wax Administration Building
1525 Howe Street
Racine, Wis. 53403
414-631-2154

Marin County Civic Center
3301 Civic Center Drive
San Rafael, Calif. 94901
415-499-6646

Taliesin
Highway 23 and County Road C.
Spring Green, Wis. 53588
608-588-7900

Taliesin West
Cactus Rd. and Frank Lloyd Wright Blvd.
Scottsdale, Ariz. 85261
480-860-8810

MORE BOOKS TO READ

Davis, Frances A. *Frank Lloyd Wright: Maverick Architect.* Minneapolis,
    Minn.: The Lerner Publishing Group, 1996.

McDonough, Yona Z. *Frank Lloyd Wright.* Broomall, Pa.: Chelsea
    House Publishers, 1992.

Wright, David K. *Frank Lloyd Wright: Visionary Architect.* Berkeley
    Heights, N.J. : Enslow Publishers, Inc., 1999.

INDEX

Art Deco 55
Arts and Crafts Movement 22

Broadacre City 39, 42

cantilevers 7, 41
Cheney, Mamah Borthwick 24, 25, 26, 27, 28
Chicago 12, 13, 14, 15, 45
classical architecture 18, 54
Conover, Allan D. 12

Emerson, Ralph Waldo 52

Fallingwater 5, 40–41, 42, 49
Froebel, Friedrich 11

Great Depression 33, 35, 39
Guggenheim Museum 48–50
Gurdjieff, Georgei Ivanovich 34, 35, 36

Hollyhock House 30, 31, 48

Imperial Hotel, Tokyo 29, 30, 31
Industrial Revolution 22

Johnson Wax Administration Building 44

Kaufmann, Edgar J. 40, 42

Le Corbusier 32, 33, 55
Lloyd-Jones family 8, 9, 10, 11, 12

Marin County Civic Center 49, 54

Oak Park 15–17, 18, 19, 24, 25
open-plan living 7, 46
organic architecture 7, 18, 22, 43, 54

Pfeiffer, B.B. 24, 39, 43
prairie houses 20, 21, 22
Princeton principles 36

Ruskin, John 22
Russell, Bertrand 53

Silsbee, J.L. 12
skyscrapers 45–46
Sullivan, Louis 12–13, 15, 18

Taliesin 9, 26–27, 28, 30, 32, 34, 35, 36, 37, 51, 52, 54
Taliesin Fellowship 36–37, 39, 40, 42, 43, 53, 54
Taliesin Foundation 22
Taliesin West 42–43

Unitarian Meeting House 47
Unity Chapel 12, 31
Unity Temple 23
Usonian architecture 39, 45–46, 47

Villa Medici 25, 26

Ward W. Willits house 20, 21
"Wasmuth Portfolio" 25
Winslow House 18–19
Wright, Anna (mother) 8, 9, 11, 12, 15, 31
Wright, Catherine (first wife) 14–15, 17, 24, 25, 29, 30
Wright, David (son) 14, 15
Wright, Eric Lloyd (grandson) 47
Wright, Frank Lloyd
  achievements 4, 5, 6–7
  appearance and character 6, 7, 21, 23, 45, 46, 48, 52
  architectural principles 4, 7, 15, 16, 18, 19, 20, 21, 22, 33, 36, 39, 43, 49, 50, 53, 54, 55
  Autobiography 11, 13, 26, 38
  birth and early life 9, 10–11
  Celtic ancestry 9, 27
  death 50–51
  marriages and children 14–15, 17, 24, 25, 30, 32, 35
  public honors 45
  working practices 17, 37
Wright, John (son) 7, 15, 17, 30
Wright, Miriam (second wife) 28–29, 30, 31, 32, 35
Wright, Olgivanna (third wife) 33, 34, 35, 36, 38, 47, 51, 55
Wright, William Cary (father) 8, 10, 11